A Father's Final Apology

A Father's Final Apology

Amber Meece

iUniverse LLC
Bloomington

A FATHER'S FINAL APOLOGY

iUniverse books may be ordered through booksellers or by contacting:

iUniverse LLC
1663 Liberty Drive
Bloomington, IN 47403
www.iuniverse.com
1-800-Authors (1-800-288-4677)

Because of the dynamic nature of the Internet, any web addresses or links contained in this book may have changed since publication and may no longer be valid. The views expressed in this work are solely those of the author and do not necessarily reflect the views of the publisher, and the publisher hereby disclaims any responsibility for them.

Any people depicted in stock imagery provided by Thinkstock are models, and such images are being used for illustrative purposes only. Certain stock imagery © Thinkstock.

ISBN: 978-1-4917-2992-2 (sc)
ISBN: 978-1-4917-2993-9 (e)

Printed in the United States of America.

iUniverse rev. date: 03/24/2014

Chapter 1

the beginning

Annie Michael is a girl who has lost her father by suicide on 4/20/03. It has now been more than 5 years since he died; Ever since he died she has been having dreams about her dad telling her that she is married and when she asks her family about if it is true they say

"No it's just a dream."

So she believes them. It's May and school has ended so she goes to her uncles' house and spends a couple of weeks there. Her uncle showed her a storage unit that was filled of her fathers' belongings. Her uncle told her

"Anything you want you can have."

Hours pass by and she finds a box that says

"To My Family"

The box contained letters from her father to every member to the family. She searched through it and found one addressed to her. She opened it and she read

3/20/03 Dear Annie,

I was horrible to you when you were in my custody. I'm sorry very much. To show how sorry I am I gave you five husbands named: 1.Dominic Stevens, 2.Richard west, 3. Hayden Wright, 4. Jackson Mason, 5.Daniel Gresham. You may know them as Dommy, Ricky, Haydee, Dan-Dan, and Jay-Jay. I have their recent addresses since they promise never to move to another address.

Dominic Stevens
3011 Titanic Rd.
London, England 30117
0151—555-2646

Richard West
123 Ave A
New York City, New York 70214
714-555-9353

Hayden Wright
125 Ave A
New York City, New York 70214
714-555-9355

Daniel Gresham
3013 Titanic Rd.
London, England 30117
0151—555-2648

Jackson Mason
4817 Texas Rd.
Austin, Texas
216-555-3669

They all know that you exist and you will contact them and that they will address you as their wife; they also know your birthday and after I'm gone they'll be expecting you to contact them. They all promise to love, care, and respect you like I should have done from the very beginning. Again I'm very sorry.

Ronnie Michael

Chapter 2

I want the truth!

Annie was in shock! She was constantly asking her family if it was true and they all lied to her. She was really confused. She storms out of the storage unit and shows her uncle the letter. He was also in major shock and very confused.

"The letter has their recent addresses and phone numbers and since they promised never to move you can contact them when you are home; they are expecting you to contact them yourself. Call your mom and tell her what you have found and if she needs proof from me I will talk to her.

Chapter 3

Hello . . . . ?

Annie has now been home for a few days and has been staring at the phone in her room. She was thinking are they awake, what do they look like, do they really love me? She read the letter again; picked up the phone and dialed a number. No answer but she left a message saying.

"This is Annie Michael and I'm calling for Daniel the time is 12 noon at Louisville, KY in the United States call me back at 1-502-555-9373 bye."

After that phone call she got paranoid but she called Jackson, Dominic, and Richard but, no answer. She called Hayden and he answered. She told him who she was and he started to cry. Both were really happy he told her

"I have really missed you for a long time and so have the others." Hayden admitted.

"I called the others but they didn't answer so I left a message on their machines." Annie added.

"I've talked to them not too long ago; I'll tell them that you have contacted me and you are having trouble contacting them." Hayden added.

"Ok." She agreed.

"I love you my wife." Hayden said.

"I love you too." Annie got all happy and giggly.

The other four called her and told her the exact same thing that Hayden had told her. They all agreed to come back to Louisville, KY to have a reunion.

Chapter 4

the reunion

Annie is scared and nervous. The reunion is going to take place in the parking lot of her school. When he saw her husbands' she was amazed she thought

"Is this a dream or a joke or am I dead? Because there is no way I'm seeing my favorite actors in person."

Annie got out of the car and Daniel reintroduced all five husbands'.

"It's us Annie Dan-Dan, Dommy, Haydee, Ricky, and Jay-Jay."

They all agreed to move together in London after Annie had graduated high school.

Chapter 5

the new school year

8/21/09 Dear Diary in 2 days the new school year starts and all of my husbands' have called to talk to me and check on me and they also say to come and visit me at school for lunch and that they say that they love me and they will show me how much they do.

The school year went fine but, with the fear of spilling the beans with anyone became difficult. Christmas break comes and they all sent their presents and spent the holidays with their families and told them that they have been reunited with their young wife.

It's time to go back to school the husbands' go to school and check on her and tell her how much they love her.

Spring Break comes and the husbands' come to Louisville to spend her week of freedom from school with her. The husbands have been talking about whose baby she should have first. They all agreed that she should have Dominic's' baby. The others kissed her and hugged her and told her they loved her.

Chapter 6

the first night

Dominic started to come towards Annie and he touched, kiss her and more. Then she started to do the same. They became intimately and passionate. An hour later they were worn out so they cuddled and kissed each other. They both thought of the results of the night and how their life would change.

Chapter 7

waiting

Two days have passed since the night that Annie and Dominic became connected. Both Dominic and Annie are wondering if to and when to buy pregnancy tests. Dominic rushed out of the hotel room to buy 10 different tests. 20 minutes later the results came back. All 10 tests came out positive! Both were very happy but, then a thought came to Annie's mind.

"What about my other husbands, do they know that I also love them too with the same amount that I love Dominic? Maybe I should have gotten some protection? I'm not sure but I am happy that I am with child."

Chapter 8

telling the news

4/3/10 Dear Diary I'm 16 and I'm expecting my first child with my oldest husband Dominic Stevens who is in his 30s. I don't know how to tell my family and my other 4 husbands.

Annie has called a family meeting with her husbands'.

"Husbands' I'm pregnant with Dominic's baby but I want all of you to know that I do love all of you equally."

Chapter 9

regret

That night Annie went to bed but, didn't go to sleep because she thought she was having a baby too early. Also not being able to show the other husbands' the same love that she showed Dominic. Morning came and Annie called another meeting.

"Daniel, Jackson, Hayden, and Richard I want to spend private time with all of you equally."

"Ok"

They all agreed.

Chapter 10

time alone and coping

Richard had Annie first. They got to know each other a little more. She did the same thing with the other husbands'.

4/8/10 Dear Diary School is going back in session soon and I'm pregnant, I've been out of school in a week and I'm coming back pregnant! What will my friends and teachers think? I'm worried that I will get into a fight and get pushed down the stairs and lose the baby and that will make Dominic and me very unhappy.

Chapter 11

Annie's decision

Annie talked to her husbands' about her worries.

"Don't worry; if you are this worried about the health and life of our baby then you'll move to England and live with me until we find a house that all of us can live in."

Later Dominic talked to the other husbands' about Annie's worries and the idea that Dominic came up with. They all agreed on Dominic's' decision on calming their young and pregnant wife.

Chapter 12

moving

4/12/10 Dear Diary I'm on a plain going to London, England to be with Dominic since I am carrying his child also I can also spend time with Daniel and his parents who also live in London, England. Later we'll find a house big enough to hold all of us and they'll all be there when I give birth.

"I can't believe that I'm in the place that I have always wanted to be at. I'm so happy!" Annie says with excitement.

"Calm down honey we'll be at my apartment soon." Dominic insisted.

"Good I need to rest." Annie said with relief.

"Good I have been wondering if you have been resting." Dominic was relieved that his young bride was resting.

As soon as they walked through the door Annie asked.

"Where is the bedroom?"

"In the back" Dominic replied.

Both Dominic and Daniel were waiting for her to wake up. As soon as they saw her entering the living room they both kissed her and touched her pregnant belly. All of them smiled.

"Daniel will be working on a movie and I might get a job soon as well so you need to stay here and take care of you and the baby; if you need fresh air then go outside in the backyard and be careful going down the stairs. You are not allowed to go anywhere out of this house except the back yard since you are new to the country. Ok?"

"Ok" Annie says with much agreement.

Annie spent the days on the internet looking for a house to hold her, 5 husbands', and all the kids soon to come.

"Oh wow I think I found it!" She reads.

"This house has 11 bedrooms, huge backyard, 4 car garage, front deck, 3 bathrooms (one on each level), 3 levels, living room, Dining room, a huge basement. The price is 1500 house is 2 years old."

"I love it!" she says with much joy.

A few hours later Daniel comes to check on her. She is excited for one of her husbands' is here to hear the news. She shows him what she found on the internet. He was also happy that she found a house that everyone could live in. A few more minutes later Dominic came home and Daniel and Annie showed him what Annie had found.

"Good I'll call a meeting to tell the brother husbands' what you found."

The next day they had a meeting over the phone about the house that Annie, Daniel, and Dominic fell in love with.

They all loved it! Dominic called the real estate agent to buy the house. In one day they all owned the house of their dreams.

A week later they moved in. two weeks later everyone was settled.

Chapter 13

life, pregnant, and in London

4/16/10 Dear Diary I'm in the place that I love more than my home town and country and I can't go anywhere to see what I have always wanted to see because I'm expecting. I'm so angry but, they all love me and they all are worried but, they couldn't allow me to have a little more freedom? They are so strict.

Annie called another meeting telling how she feels.

"I want to walk Daniels' dogs Jake and Amy; all three of us needs some exercise."

"I think you are right. You need to do something other than watching the T.V. and Jake and Amy also need exercise too. Yes you can walk them but not too far from the house." Daniel and the other husbands agreed

Chapter 14

the new lifestyle

4/18/10 Dear Diary the new lifestyle is good and the new house is wonderful! Daniel Dogs love the walks and best of all they don't chase wild animals also I love the exercise and the fresh air.

When she came back she saw a bouquet of flowers with a card saying

"I love you so much and I can't wait to raise our baby with you.

Love Dominic"

She sighs. "I'm doing a good job. I'm making him very happy!" She thinks to herself.

Chapter 15

love is in the air

Annie woke up with no warning to see all her husbands' just staring at her as if she was Snow White in a deep sleep. They all had a different bouquet of flowers.

"What's up guys'? What is it?" She asked.

"We are going to take you to the sites that you have wanted to go to since the day you came to England." Replied Richard.

"Are you guys serious? Is this for real?"

"Yes!" They all replied.

They went to the sites. Annie enjoyed the time that she and all her husband's shared.

Chapter 16

the pregnancy

7/20/10 Dear Diary I'm now 3 and half months pregnant. I'm having morning sickness but Doctor Stephens said the baby will be a healthy baby. Why do they call it morning sickness if you can have it at any time of day? Dominic is glowing and is happy and the rest of my husbands' can't wait to have kid of their own so they can feel the great pride and joy that Dominic is feeling. We don't know the gender of the baby yet. In 2 months we might know the gender.

7/20/10 Dear Diary this is Dominic and my first journal entry. I don't know how I should start this. It's noon here in London, England and my wife is having morning sickness. Why do they call it morning sickness if you can have it anytime of the day? My brother husbands' and I can't wait for this baby! They will also have a child of their own later on. I feel much pride and joy!

Chapter 17

shopping

7/21/10 Dear Diary this is Daniel this is my first journal entry. Today Annie, my brother husbands' and I went shopping for the baby to come in a matter of months. I hope we don't go overboard especially me for I am an only child and never got the chance to go shopping for a baby.

"How adorable is this little tiny baby items!"

Says Daniel.

Chapter 18

wishing

7/23/10 Dear Diary we are all wishing for a girl. As for Daniel is wondering why parents didn't have any more kids. Everyone is learning how to take care of a baby and is scared to be a horrible parent. Today is also Daniel's birthday!

7/23/10 Dear Diary its Jackson my wife is constantly thinking about our future with all 5 of her husbands' having a baby of our own. She looks beautiful and Daniel is wondering about his life with siblings if he has any and he might be the last husband to have a baby; he is the youngest of the 5 husbands'.

Chapter 19

the baby is going to be a . . . .

7/25/10 Dear Diary the baby is due in February, 3ʳᵈ 2011 the baby will be a girl! Yay I get a little girl but, the doctor could be wrong. My doctor said I would be a boy well I guess I showed them when I came out a girl.

7/30/10 Dear Diary the baby will be a girl. My daughter will come on February, 3ʳᵈ 2011. It's now July so we have some time to pick out a name.

"Husbands', meeting now!" Yelled Annie

"Have any of you got a list of names?" Annie says in calm voice.

No one answered.

"Well I would like all of you to make a list. I will look at all of them and choose a name for first and middle" Annie announced.

They all rushed to different places in the house to do their lists.

Dominic	Daniel	Jackson	Richard	Hayden	Finals
Sophie	Marcia	Alice	Elle	Padme	Rosie
Rosie	Emma	Esme	Kristen	Natalie	Marcia
Tanya	Bonnie	Renee	Nessa	Leia	Carlie
Donna		Carlie		Carrie	Padme
					Elle

8/5/10 Dear Diary we five husbands' like what our wife asked us to do to choose a first and middle name for the baby.

Chapter 20

waiting for the day

"When will the day come?" Annie complains all the time.

"Now calm down sweetie the baby will some when she is ready." Dominic tries to calm his young wife down.

"It feels like I have been pregnant for 5 long years." Annie added.

"We all want this baby to come and she will come." Dominic continues to calm down Annie.

8/20/10 Dear Diary I want my daughter now! I know I'm driving all my husbands' crazy because I'm constantly saying it.

8/21/10 Dear Diary this is all 5 husbands' we have all noticed that our wife has stopped complaining since she last wrote in her journal. We think that she sensed our frustration with her complaining about her being pregnant.

8/23/10 Dear Diary All of my husbands' has been giving me questions like did u lose the baby, did you sense our frustration? I told them the truth and to assure them that I was telling the truth I said go with me to my next appointment and there they will do an ultrasound.

8/23/10 Dear Diary its Dominic we have all asked Annie the questions and she said she'll take me with her to her next appointment where they will do an ultrasound.

8/30/10 Annie is still pregnant! I'm so happy!

9/2/10 Dear Diary all of my husbands' are happy that I'm still pregnant. Dominic is acting like a crazy person well he is the father after all.

Chapter 21

the year goes by . . . .

Home school is still in session for Annie. The date is 9/12/10 and everyone is anxious and worried about the baby and Annie. The morning sickness continues.

9/4/10 Dear Diary everything is fine but, my husbands' are becoming a pain in the behind.

It's now October 31ˢᵗ also known as Halloween everyone is worried about me giving birth months early and its Friday too; Dominic apparently never told me how superstitious he was.

Now it's thanksgiving everyone is anxious because the month is coming.

Now it's December 24ᵗʰ. Annie is anxious for what kind of baby things she'll get for Christmas. Morning comes and Annie gets lots and lots of baby things.

Chapter 22

the baby is coming

"Ow" screamed Annie.

"I think she's coming!" Annie screamed again.

"Her water just broke!" Screamed Jackson.

"Get the car ready!" Yelled Dominic.

10 minutes later they got to the hospital. 15 minutes later Carlie was born.

Carlie Sophie Stevens
6 IB 6 OZ
Dr. Gary Stephen
Red Cross Hospital
1/5/11 2:00 P.M.
London, England

1/7/11 Dear Diary Dominic and I are now parents! My other husbands' are father/uncles'. I will show my new daughter love and care. Carlie came early so she has to stay in the hospital longer than me. I'm a little weak from giving birth but, at my age it is to be expected.

1/7/11 Dear Diary its Dominic I'm now a father! All of us will show Carlie love and will care for her and we'll do the same with our wife who is very weak from giving birth at her age. Annie can come home when she gets her strength back; she lost some blood while giving birth. Carlie came really early so she can't come home until she gets some weight on her.

Chapter 23

Coming home

"Annie is coming home soon Jackson" Richard announced.

"I know" replied Jackson.

"But, Carlie has to stay in the hospital longer than Annie because she was born early" Richard added.

"Yes we all know" said everyone very frustrated.

"Richard we all want both mother and daughter home now!" Hayden added.

1/11/11 Dear Diary I'm going home tomorrow but, without my new daughter. She has to stay here at the hospital until she gets more weight. I hope my husbands' have tended to the nursery; when I get home I'm going to put some of my touches on the room.

"Ok babe we have all of your stuff in the trunk of the car. Are you ready?" Dominic asked.

"Can we go see Carlie before we leave" Annie asked.

"Of course and one of us will call on her condition ok?" replied Richard.

They all go to the nursery in the hospital. Carlie smiles when she sees her mother and Annie tears up. Annie talks to Carlie.

"Hi sweetie we all love you and we'll call on how you are doing."

Annie really starts to cry when she going towards the door to the car. 10 minutes later they are home and Annie goes straight to the nursery and cries more because her daughter is not with her. Dinner time came and it was quiet. You could hear a pen drop. Everyone was expecting for the hospital to call and say your baby can come home or hear her cry as If she came home with Annie. Carlie was a premature baby like her mother.

Chapter 24

Carlie's homecoming

"Ring Ring" goes the phone.

"Hello?" Hayden answered.

"Is this the home of Carlie Stevens?"

"Yes it is." Hayden replied.

"Carlie is ready to come home! You can pick her up on the maternity floor of the hospital." Says the nurse.

"Ok we'll be there soon thank you." Hayden felt relieved.

"Guys that was the hospital they said Carlie can come home!" Hayden announced.

"Are you serious?" Annie asked.

"Yes check the caller ID" Hayden added.

She did and Hayden was telling the truth.

"Dominic come on our daughter can come home!" Annie ordered.

"I'm coming" Dominic yells.

Everyone is very excited and anxious. They went to where the nurse said to go to claim Carlie. 50 Minutes later they were all home. Annie put Carlie in the nursery as soon as they came into the house. She put her down into the crib and as soon as her little body felt the soft bed she fell asleep. Annie quietly and quickly put the batteries into the baby monitor and turned it on and left the room. Every 5 minutes someone checked in on her and if she made a noise they all ran to the nursery.

Chapter 25

the new member of the family

Carlie was quiet. She was no trouble at all. She only cried when she needed something. Annie got a little worried that she was not loud but when she looked at her baby books she reads.

"Some babies cry a lot and some cry very little. It is nothing to worry about."

Chapter 26

Can we talk?

2/2/11 Dear Diary it's Richard today it could have been Carlie's birthday but, she came early. In 3 days she will be a month old. My brother husbands' and I have been having secret meetings about when I should try to conceive with our wife Annie. I've been thinking that it's too early for her; she is in her teen years of age and she still might be weak from giving birth. I think I'll talk to Annie in private without anyone knowing.

"Annie may I talk to you in private?" Asked Richard.

"Sure" she walks in a room with him.

"What about?" she asked.

"Us having a baby" He added.

"OK continue" said Annie was very curious of what he is going to say.

"I want to know when you feel like conceiving again so I will not mess up your reproductive organs." Richard said with terror.

"Well give me a few more weeks and we'll see how I feel." Annie announced.

"Ok thanks." Richard felt very much relieved.

Weeks went by and Annie was feeling good and was ready to continue her duties as a wife/mother. When it was Richard's night she surprised him by getting really friendly and she told him.

"I'm ready!"

They did it for an hour and cuddled and wondered about what will this night bring for them. Richard felt really good about what he did and he felt good about the way he approached Annie about the situation of making him a father.

Chapter 27

waiting again

It has now been 2 days since the surprised night so Richard went out and bought 10 pregnancy tests'. When the results came back 5 of them were positive and the other 5 were negative. They were shocked and scared.

"I don't know what is going on; I'll go to the doctor to see the true results were they can do a real test. Just be calm until I get an appointment and no matter what the results will be we are going to be fine." Annie said trying to get things straight and calm her husband down.

Richard was going crazy he thought that he messed up her reproductive organs or they were no longer working; he went into a panic/anxiety attack.

Chapter 28

the Dr. Appointment

"Well Mrs. Michael's what seems to be the problem with you today?" Asked Dr. Pope.

"Well I'm trying to have another baby and the father went out to buy those pregnancy tests that they have in the drugstores and he bought 10 and half was positive and the other half was negative. So I want you to run a real test to see the real results."

"Ok" the doctor did what the patient wanted.

The staff did a lot tests'. 15 minutes later the results came back. The results were mixed matched again but, there were more positives' than negatives.

"We'll keep an eye on the results; they might change; if anything changes we will contact you."

"Thank you." Annie felt good that her doctor assured her.

Days later the Doctors' office called.

"Mrs. Michael's you are defiantly pregnant!"

"Thank you so much for calling!" Annie felt very greatful for the wonderful news!

"Husbands' I have some news!" Annie yelled.

"I'm pregnant! But, I feel different.

the big surprise

2/18/11 Dear Diary the pregnancy is normal; morning sickness and all but, I feel strange it feels like I'm carrying more than one baby. Well I'll go to the doctor to see how it's going.

"Hey DR. Pope I feel strange. I think I might be carrying more than one baby."

"Well let's see what's going on." Said the doctor.

The doctor put Annie on an ultrasound machine. There was a big surprise!

"Wow . . . . You are carrying twins!"

"Twins wow!"

3/1/11 Dear Diary I'm carrying twins! I will tell my husbands' soon!

"Husbands' I'm carrying twins!"

All the husbands' fell to the floor. A few hours later they woke up and they went to the places where they hidden their journals.

3/4/11 Dear Diary its Richard I'm going to be a father to twins! We all just woke up from falling to the floor when she told us the news. Luckily no one landed on Carlie she was away from the area were we all felled.

3/4/11 Dear Diary I told my husbands' and they fell to the floor. Gladly no one got hurt; Carlie was far away from my husbands'; she was in her automatic swing in a corner near me. I'm happy she was safe from being crushed.

Chapter 30

Another list for baby names

After they all got better and finished their journal entries Annie asked them.

"I need a list of both boy and girl names"

They did that during private time where they read a book. The next day in the afternoon they all gave her their lists' of both boy and girl names.

Girl

Dominic	Jackson	Daniel	Richard	Hayden	Finals
Donna	Bella	Emma	Elle	Padme	Elle
Rosie	Esme	Katie	Kristen	Leia	Padme
Tanya	Renee				Bella

Boy

Dominic	Jackson	Daniel	Richard	Hayden	Finals
Sky	Jasper	Matt	Warner	Anakin	Sky
Peter	Allen	Devon	Glen	Luke	Jasper
					Matt
					Warner
					Anakin

Chapter 31

the pregnancy

4/3/11 Dear Diary I'm having morning sickness and I hate it but, it's a sign that the babies will be healthy. In 2 weeks I will know the genders of the babies.

4/25/11 Dear Diary the genders are one boy and a girl. All I have to do now is choose which baby name I really like. The due date is 11/11/11 and they'll be born at the same hospital as Carlie.

Chapter 32

the worst time ever!

One night Annie was up all night with morning sickness, all of her husbands' had food poisoning, and Carlie was crying because she could not some sleep because, all of the parents' throwing up.

A week later the husbands' got better so they went to a lawyers' office, told their story, and sued the restaurant where they all got sick.

4/4/11 Dear Diary my husbands' are suing the restaurant where they got sick, they are asking for 1,000,000 dollars because I'm pregnant with twins, I have a 3 month old baby, I was also throwing up while they were throwing up too so no one was able to take care of Carlie very well. I hope we win the case.

4/4/11 Dear Diary it's all of the husbands' we are suing the restaurant that made us all sick. While we were all throwing up our wife was throwing up too. Carlie didn't get her three A.M. feeding and her diaper didn't get changed either.

The date is 4/18/11 and it is the day of the trial. Everyone is worried and wondering if they will win or lose.

"Well since you got really sick so sick that you all couldn't tend to a 3 month old. You should get the money you asked." The judge ordered.

4/20/11 Dear Diary we won the case! I'm so happy!

4/20/11 Dear Diary its Dominic we won the case!

The next night everyone watched the news.

"The restaurant Good Fish and Chips is now permanently closed for 2 reasons they had toxic/poisonous liquid which makes food poisoning and they lost a law suit and got bankrupted. The owners are in jail on a life sentence!"

The next 5 minutes everyone was in shock. Not only were they in shock the entire continent was in shock too. The restaurant was a big and popular place to get fish and chips and any one could have gotten sick. Days later everyone was happy that the restaurant lost the case, put in jail on a life sentence, and might be killed for possible murder.

4/30/11 Dear Diary I have a doctor appointment soon I'm resting, watching T.V., reading books and magazines.

the twins progress

"Hey Mrs. Michaels how have you been feeling?"

"I have had some sickness and I won a lawsuit." Announced Annie

"I know I heard." The doctor was amazed.

The doctor turned on the ultrasound machine and found something that does not happen a lot!

"Mrs. Michaels your twins are conjoined also known as connected." The Doctor announced.

"What how can this happen?" Annie was shocked and surprised.

"There is an operation to separate them but, they need to be strong or one or both will die." The doctor announced.

On the way home many thoughts came into Annie's' mind.

Will they both die or live or will one of the die or live? Will they share organs? How did they get connected? Were they connected when we found out the genders'? Could they each have one arm? All of the questions worried and scared her. Most importantly she didn't know how to tell Richard.

Chapter 34

telling Richard

Tonight was Richards' night to sleep with Annie so she was going to tell him. Throughout the day Annie was scared about his reaction and more. Dinner came and all of the husbands' asked Annie about what the doctor said she answered no one.

Bed time came and Annie watched Richard turn on the T.V. and flip through the channels. She opened her mouth and talked.

"Richard I want to tell you something about the babies."

Richard gave Annie his absolute attention.

"The doctor saw something unusual. The babies are conjoined also known as connected. The doctor said there might be a way to separate them."

Richard started to stutter and was in shock.

"How could have this had happen?"

Both didn't get any sleep that night. The next day Richard called his dad.

"Dad I have some news about my twin babies. The doctor said that they are conjoined!"

There was a pause.

"Richard I didn't want to tell you; you had a twin brother named Eric you and him were conjoined. We had the operation to have you separated from him but during the operation the doctors' found out that one of you was weak. They continued with it; Eric died during it. Your mother and I were depressed when we found out what happened. Eric had a weak heart and you didn't so that's why you survived."

Richard was once again in shock!

4/7/11 Dear diary its Richard today I found out that I was a twin and that we were connected to each other. We went through the separation operation. Eric my brother had a weak heart so he died but, I didn't have a weak heart so here I am. Maybe that's why my kids are connected. I'll tell my wife soon.

4/7-8/11 Dear Diary in the middle of the night Richard told me about him being a twin and how he and his brother were conjoined and his brother Eric had a weak heart so he died in the middle of the operation. Richard wonders why his parents didn't tell him about this until now but, at least now we know why the babies are connected.

Chapter 35

the strange pregnancy continues

Annie feels weird inside and outside because of the twins. She has morning sickness some days but, not all. That worries her a little.

It's now June and Annie's' belly is big and she still feel weird and she is also terrified. The months go by and she feels the same all of the time.

It's August and everyone is anxious for the twins to come.

Its September Annie is big and scared and worried about her unborn twins and in their condition.

It's October and Annie is getting tired of being pregnant.

On October 5th Annie started to have contractions! So Richard took her to the hospital. As soon as she got out of the car at the hospital her water broke!

Chapter 36

the birth

Annie started to push.

Bella and Anakin were born. Bella came out head first then she rested and started to push some more and Anakin came out feet first! When they were all the way out and the umbilical cord cut they saw they were connected by their feet!

Bella Rosie West
6 IB. 6OZ
10/5/11 1:30 A.M.
Dr. Gary Stephens
Red Cross Hospital
London, England

Anakin Matt West
6 IB. 6OZ.
10/5/11 1:33 A.M.
Dr. Gary Stephens
Red Cross Hospital
London, England

The doctor told Annie and Richard that both hearts were strong but, they wished they could do the operation anyway.

The surgery went fine. Their feet were a good baby size feet Both Anakin and Bella were alive and wonderful and their feet will be normal! Both parents were very happy!

Two weeks went by and both babies were living and doing wonderful!

Two more weeks went by and Annie was released from the hospital. Bella and Anakin were still recovering from the surgery. At home the husbands were putting the two cribs together making sure they would have 2 babies to bring home. A few more weeks went by and the twins could come home.

Chapter 37

the twins homecoming

At 11:00 the hospital called and said

"Bella and Anakin are ready to come home."

15 minutes later they were home. Bella hated Anakin and he the same. Bella was a quite girl and Anakin was always crying for something; Bella ignores her brother all the time. She only cries when she needs something.

Anakin is sick.

Anakin had a 101° temperature. The doctor said he had a very bad infected ear so they admitted him to the hospital. All parents were worried for this was the first time a young baby was very sick. Anakin was in the hospital for a month because he almost died but, he came back on his own. A day later he almost died again but, came back again on his own. The doctor called his family and said if he does not almost die again he might be able to go home in 3 weeks."

Chapter 39

Anakin's' homecoming

The 3 weeks went by and the hospital called saying Anakin could come home! Annie was very happy to hear the news even though he might cry all the time. When he came home he was sleeping and snoring; Annie was crying tears of joy for he was home and was alive. His first night he cried a few times for what he needed but, for the rest of the night he was quiet but, snoring and everybody was happy. The next morning he was quiet but, breathing. He only cried when he needed something. Everyone was very happy!

Chapter 40

the year continues

It's now December and Carlie is 11 months old and the twins are 2 months old. Everything is going good and everyone is happy. The husbands' are having meetings about when they should Annie and Hayden will conceive. They all agreed in one month they'll ask (January). Christmas is soon and Carlie is excited about her first Christmas. Carlie, Bella, and Anakin got many presents.

It's now New Years Eve and Carlie is excited for her first birthday is soon. It's now 1/5/12 and Carlie is turning one. She is very happy for this day is her day. She got many presents and her siblings had fun with her cake icing and the torn wrapping presents. That night she went to bed a year older she was happy and joyful.

Chapter 41

Annie can I have a moment with you

"Annie can I have a moment with you?" Asked Hayden.

"Sure"

They go to Haydens' room and talk.

"It's been a few months since you last gave birth and I wondered when you feel ready to conceive again. It's my turn to become a father." Hayden acknowledged.

"I think we should try on your next night." Annie insisted.

Chapter 42

Another night

1/27/12 tonight is Haydens' night and we'll try to conceive. I hope everything goes well.

1/27/12 Its Hayden tonight is my night and the night that Annie and I will try to conceive. I hope everything goes well.

Its night time and Hayden is already in his room reading a magazine. Annie heads to his room and she closes the door. They get closer to each other and they start to kiss and take off each others' clothes and they get very intendment.

An hour later both are worn out. They cuddle, kiss and fall asleep in each other's arms. Dreaming about the results.

Chapter 43

waiting again

It's been 2 days since the night so Hayden goes out to get 10 pregnancy tests. He comes home Annie opens all the tests and 20 minutes later they all say . . . . NEGATIVE!

"What!" both Annie and Hayden were in shock? They also denied the results and said

"I'm/your pregnant I/we know it."

"Make an appointment to see what is going on" Hayden demanded.

the appointment

"Hey Mrs. Michaels" says the doctor.

"Hey doc I need to know if I'm pregnant because I did them and they all said negative and I want to know if they were telling the truth."

"Well let's just see." The doctor does the pregnancy tests.

25 minutes later the results came back.

"Mrs. Michaels you . . . are NOT pregnant" the doctor announced.

Annie went into tears quickly. She didn't want to tell Hayden the bad news for they both worked hard.

Annie went home and she hid away in her room. She stayed in there all day and did not sleep with the husband that had her that night. Hayden came to her in her room to see what was wrong. She told him and he told her

"We will try again I promise."

2/5/12 Dear Diary I'm not pregnant but, Hayden and I will try again.

2/5/12 Dear Diary its Hayden Annie is not pregnant but we will try again.

Chapter 45

Another night of trying

They started the way they did before but, this time he told her

"I love you my sexy wife."

"And I love you."

Before them both knew it they did two hours of sex.

It has now been a week since the second night so this time Hayden went out and bought 20 tests this time. 30 minutes later the results came back. They all said . . . . pregnant!

"I want to go to the doctor just to be sure." Annie insisted.

"Ok." Hayden agreed.

The next day Annie got an appointment.

"Hey doc I think I'm pregnant this time because I got 20 tests and all said pregnant so here I am to see if they are telling the truth."

"Ok let's take a look." Says the doctor.

The doctor looked at the ultrasound. The doctor told her to

"Get dressed and met me in my office."

She got dressed and went to his office.

"You are pregnant!"

She went home and told Hayden. He was thrilled! Later during dinner she told the other husbands' and she also told them to make list of names for both genders because they didn't know the gender yet. After dinner the husbands' went to their rooms and made their lists for both boy and girl names.

Boy

Dominic	Jackson	Daniel	Richard	Hayden	Finals
Sky	Jasper	Devon	Warner	Luke	Sky
Peter	Allen		Glen		Jasper
					Allen

Girl

Dominic	Jackson	Daniel	Richard	Hayden	Finals
Donna	Esme	Emma	Elle	Padme	Padme
	Renee	Katie	Kristen	Natalie	Elle
	Alice	Marcia	Nessa	Carrie	Emma
				Leia	Esme

Four months later she went to the doctor and found out what the gender was.

Chapter 46

the gender is . . . .

"Mrs. Michaels the baby is a boy!"

The doctor announced.

The parents were very happy to know what they were expecting and they had names. When the parents got home Annie found the name ideas for the baby. She started to decide what the names' of the baby will be.

Chapter 47

the pregnancy

Annie had very little morning sickness but, all pregnancies are different. She was happy and glowing and can't wait for the baby to come. When she slept she still smiled for she was dreaming about her new life with her new baby soon to come.

It's now March and her belly is beginning to become big. All husbands' are taking care of her and her unborn baby, and the kids. She tries to take care of the kids but, the husbands' tell her

"Go to bed we have it all under control."

She goes into her room but, she doesn't sleep she lays there angry with the orders that her husbands' gave her and she is barely doing anything to show her husbands' and her kids that she loves them. When its Haydens' night he touches her pregnant belly and they kiss and cuddle.

3/16/12 Dear Diary I feel very loved but I'm not so sure about my kids I'm not able to show them love or take care of them because of my husbands' I'm so angry at them.

the Dr. Appointment

"The baby looks good and the due date will be 10/16/12. Come back in two months." The doctor addressed.

"Ok" the parents agreed.

Annie is glowing because she's expecting a boy by its self no other baby, they have a name, due date, and many new baby items. She was very excited for she has twins a boy and girl named Bella and Anakin and a girl named Carlie.

Chapter 49

my father is what!

A week after the Dr. Appointment the phone ringed. Annie answered it.

"Hi I'm police officer Charles Close and I'm calling for a relative for a man named Ronnie Michael, he is in our custody for murdering a Mr. Greene for marrying his wife Helen."

"Sir, I'm afraid that you are mistaken my father is dead he committed suicide in spring of 2003." Annie replied.

"Ma'am Your father faked his death. Before you say another no he's dead how about you come to the station and try to identify him yourself." The officer debated.

"Ok I will." Annie was desperate to prove her point.

A day later she went to the station and she identified the man that they had in their custody. She saw him in a two-way mirror and saw that this man was her father.

"I'll come back in a few days and I'll have some questions that my father should know and if he answered all of the questioned right then I will admit that this man if my father."

The police officers' agreed to her idea.

Chapter 50

the questions and the questioning

1. Where did my mom's water break at?
    In front of the ER doors at suburban Hospital on July 13, 1993 at 11:00 at night.

2. What time I born?
    11:13 at night.

3. What is my mother's name?
    Karen.

4. When and where did you marry my mom?
    September 23, 1990 in the basement if the house that we bought together.

5. What were your parent's names?
    Elmer Michaels and Anna Spears

6. When and where were you born and what was the doctor's name?
    December 2, 1958. Dr. William at St. Jacob hospital Louisville, KY.

7. Did you give me husbands'?
      Yes but, not one five.

If got last one right 8. What were their names?
      1. Dominic Stevens 2.Richard West
      3.Hayden Wright 4. Daniel Gresham
      5. Jackson Mason.

9. Do you know who I am?
      My daughter Annie.

The next day she went back to the police station and asked the man the questions.

"I'm here to ask you some questions to see if you are who you say you are ok?" Annie addressed.

"Ok" he replied.

She started to ask the questions

1. Correct
2. Correct
3. Correct
4. Correct
5. Correct
6. Correct
7. Correct
8. Correct

Before she knew it she was on the last question and he had gotten the other questions correct so she asked him the last one.

"Do you know who I am?" She asked.

He started to cry.

"Yes you are my daughter Annie."

Then she started to cry and then she started to hit him multiple times.

"Why did you fake your death?" She asked with a lot of anger.

"I was such a horrible father to you so I faked my death so you wouldn't look or talk to me and bring me down with what I did to you." He replied with fear.

"I don't know if I should put you back into my life for what you just did and/or for what you are charged for. Is there anything buried in your supposed grave?"

"A dog is buried at my supposed grave. I didn't want you to know that I was alive I wanted you to think that I was dead and that I would never hurt you or you would never have to see my face. I did give you 5 husbands like I said in my letter they all love you the way I should have loved you but I didn't so I did what I did. I could watch you live your life without the worry of me ruining your joy. I also see that you are pregnant what is gender of the baby?"

"I don't want you to know the gender but, do you know my kids names?" Annie asked.

"No when you call them I try to forget their names so I would not come to them or for you to see me I have a court date you can be there if you want to be." Her father replied.

"I don't know how to tell my husbands' that you are alive and it will be hard to keep it from my kids."

4/20/12 Dear Diary my father is alive and he has a court date for the following charges–breaking and entering, attempted murder, and faking his death. I don't know what to do with him and how to tell my husbands and try to keep this from my very young kids.

4/20/12 Dear Diary this is Ronnie my daughter now knows that I'm alive which means that I faked my death I have a court date and she might be there it's her decision if she does not know what to do with me.

Later Annie told her husbands' that her father had faked his death and not to tell the kids. The next day the kids were at Daniels' parent's house and Annie and her husbands' went to the police station. All of her husband's gave him hell. Annie had called her Uncle John and he came and saw his brother Ronnie who he also thought was dead. Her uncle asked Ronnie a question.

"Who is buried in between mom and dad?" he asked.

"A dog that I loved very much."

Her uncle could not stay in London for long so he went back to Louisville, KY and digged up the ashes of a dog.

Chapter 51

the trial

Ronnie got 3 months in jail and 3 more months for community service and during the community service he would live in a mental hospital for therapy and a place to live. Everyone was very happy with the results.

On 10/16/12 At 10:00 in the morning Annie's water broke. At 12:30 Jasper Sky Wright was born.

Jasper Sky Wright
9 IB. 9OZ.
Dr. Gary Stephens
10/16/12 12:30 P.M.
Red Cross Hospital
London, England

An hour later the family came to see Jasper. Carlie, Bella, and Anakin got Jasper presents', balloons, and for their mother a kiss and a fabric flower. The doctor told the family that Jasper would have to stay in the hospital for two weeks and Annie one week.

Chapter 52

Jaspers homecoming

Two weeks had passed and it was time to take Jasper home. Everyone was at home putting the finishing touches while waiting for the phone call from the hospital. While he was home he was half the time crying and half the time quiet as can be. Once again there was joy in the house.

A month went by and it was now time for Jackson to become a father. Jackson pulled Annie aside to ask is she was up to the task. She answered

"In a month."

Jackson became calm for that moment was over and done with.

Chapter 53

the night and the results

A month has passed and in a few nights it would be Jacksons' night. Annie and Jackson ask each other how they were doing and if they are willing to do it.

Tonight is the night. Annie and Jackson got intimate when the sun went down. Two days later Jackson went out to get the pregnancy tests'. As soon as he came back with the tests Annie did them right away; 20 minutes later the results came back. They all came out POSITIVE! Annie thought that she would tell everyone at dinner and tell Jackson that the results have not come back yet.

A few hours later Dinner time came. There was quiet moment so Annie said.

"I'm pregnant! I would like lists for boy and girl names."

It took a moment to get a response but, everyone was happy! After dinner they all went to do the lists'

Boy

Dominic	Richard	Hayden	Jackson	Daniel	Finals
Peter	Josh	Justin	Harry	Devon	Devon
					Harry
					Peter

Girl

Dominic	Jackson	Hayden	Richard	Daniel	Finals
Sarah	Alice	Jessica	Nessa	Emma	Nessa
					Sarah
					Jessica

Four weeks later Annie had a Doctors' appointment.

"The baby is doing fine; come back in two or four weeks to find out what the gender is."

The Doctor ordered.

Annie is doing well she is having some morning sickness and she rests a lot.

It was time for the doctors' appointment.

"The baby is a girl! She is due on 9/14/13." The doctor announced.

Once again there was joy and excitement at home.

Chapter 54

Change is in the air

Annie is glowing; the husbands' are happy and excited; the kids are growing and Carlie is beginning school; Daniel is relieved that he is next to become a father; he really starts to show her that he really loves her. Minutes later the phone rings.

"Hello" Annie Answers.

"Hello my beautiful daughter." Said the person on the other end of the phone.

"How did you get this number?" she asked.

"The Police officer put the number in my who to contact in case of an emergency file."

"Ok what do you want?" she asked.

"Just wondering how you are doing and more."

She told him what he wanted to hear and then they ended the phone call.

Annie is glowing with a little morning sickness. She is three months into the pregnancy; Jackson is thrilled, anxious, and is constantly day dreaming about the baby and the life they will have. The kids are also excited especially Carlie for she loves having sister but not fond on brothers for sisters are kind and sweet and brothers are mean and not at all sweet. She is constantly saying

"Girls rule and boys drool except for daddy he rules."

Every time she says that Dominic smiles when she says the end it always surprises him that she says that; he never expects it.

It's July 13, 2013 and today is Annie's birthday; she turns 20 year old. Annie is amazed on how much work she has done. She is carrying her 5th child and she is done with school and the baby will be born in a few months.

It's now August. In one month the baby will be born; everyone is anxious and excited.

the birth

On 9/14/13 Annie woke up with pain. Five minutes later her water broke. Ten minutes later she was at the hospital. Five minutes later Jessica Sarah Mason was born

Jessica Sarah Mason
9/14/13 11:13 A.M.
8 IB. 8 OZ.
Dr. Gary Stephens
Red Cross Hospital
London, England

Jessica was a very quiet baby she only cried when she needed something. Two weeks went by and Jessica and Annie were able to go home.

Chapter 54 the homecoming

At 1:00 in the afternoon everyone arrived home. As soon as Jackson, Annie and Jessica walked through the door Jackson carried his new daughter in his arms to the girls' room. Jessica started to cry so he checked her diaper it was clean so he yelled

"I need a bottle!"

Two minutes later Carlie came with a bottle and she stayed there watching her new sister getting fed. As soon as she stopped feeding she got a little fussy which meant she needed to burp. She burped and Carlie went crazy. Jackson was putting her into the crib when Carlie asked

"Can I kiss her?"

"Yes but on the forehead."

She nodded her head yes.

He slowly got down to her level and she gave Jessica a soft adorable kiss on the forehead. Then he slowly got back up to his level and put Jessica in her crib. As soon as her back felt the soft mattress she closed her eyes and slept.

Dinner came and Annie went to check on Jessica; she was awake.

"Hi sweetie did you have a good nap?"

Annie picked her up and brought her to the main level. Annie put Jessica in a motorized swing on a low speed near the eating area. Annie and Jackson had a close eye on her but Carlie had a closer eye on her. Carlie was at Jessica's side every moment she could get. Annie began to worry if Jessica was getting scared with a person starring at her most of the time. Ten minutes later Jessica started to cry Annie tended to her. As soon as she calmed down she fed her and as soon as she stopped she got burped and was put back down then Carlie rushed to her sisters' side and Jessica started to cry again. Annie's worry came true. Everyone tried to keep Carlie occupied with something so that Jessica would have some space to breathe. Finally after everyone took aspirins for their headaches Annie tucked Carlie in for bed. Annie talked about how Jessica was constantly crying when she was around her. Carlie understood what mom was saying to her so they made an agreement. That Carlie should only be near her sister when anyone needs help with anything that deals with Jessica like giving a clean diaper to the person changing the diaper or bring another bottle.

the visit to the ER

On Halloween Daniel came home from work with chest pains. Annie was really worried so she called for an ambulance. When they came they put Daniel on a gurney and suddenly he closed his eyes. Everyone was behind the ambulance in the family car. When they got to the hospital his heart began to beat slowly. Annie rushed to the nurses' station to see the condition on Daniel the nurse called for anyone who was working on Daniel. A nurse came down to the waiting room and told them

"Daniel is having a heart attack he is going to surgery as we speak. He will be having an angioplasty it's a repair of a blood vessel by putting a metal stint to unblock arteries. In a few hours he will be in the intensive care unit for a number of days then he'll be in a regular room for some weeks and then he'll be home can't do a lot of work just needs to lay around and be calm no stress but, during home he'll have some physical therapy at a local clinic."

"Thank you for all of your help." Annie was grateful.

the visit

Two days later the family saw Daniel. Annie was scared about her youngest husband's health like will he be able to conceive or have sex after our first child, to chase down our child to take a bath and more. Annie tried her best not to cry for that would be stress for him for it was his choice to smoke which caused the heart attack. She gave him a hug and a kiss on the forehead and asked him

"How are you feeling?"

"Scared" he replied

He starts to get upset and saying

"It's my fault; I'm the reason why I'm here"

"Calm down you are here and alive and recovering, I'm here but, the kids will not come because you need to be calm and have no stress."

Annie calmed her husband.

"I came through for you and the life that we have. Annie I love you Don't think that the only way that you can make me happy is by giving me a child, our child it's not; you and the guys already make me happy; I have brothers'/husbands, your kids that are my nieces/ nephews/1 third mine, and most important you. I quit smoking when I'm stressed I'll do something to relieve my stress; no smoking and that is final." Daniel preached.

Annie starts to blush and begins to feel grateful for the life and for what she has.

Two weeks later Daniel was moved to a regular Hospital room. Two more weeks later Daniel was in outpatient therapy for three months where he did small exercise steps. He was home doing what the doctor prescribed lying around when he was not doing therapy. He was in his room throughout the day and at dinner he was with the family eating the kids were calm during dinner and while he was in his room his door was closed so the kids would run around and not disturb him and they had an intercom setting on their phone so if he needed something he used the intercom and Annie or one of his brother/husbands' would come in close the door give him what he needed if he wanted to talk they would stay when they left they closed the door behind them and made sure it was all the way closed. After that three month time period he had to wait to have sex. The date is now 3/17/2014 and Daniel was ready to have sex but, the doctors thought different. Two weeks (4/28/2014) later the doctors' told him to take it step by step and a month later (5/28/2014) the doctors said

"yes but not rough at all."

Daniel agreed after all he was an actor and the doctors' were medical experts. Another month later both Daniel and the doctors said yes you are now able to have fully fledged sex. Two nights later (5/30/2014) it was Daniels night so they did it. Two days later (6/1/2014) Daniel asked Dominic to go and get the pregnancy tests'. Five minutes later he was back with the tests'. Ten minutes later the results came back. She was pregnant! Suddenly she began to worry about how Daniels' heart will react to the wonderful news so she told him calmly. He reacted well his heart was calm so he didn't go into shock; she was relieved. Later at dinner she told the rest of the family. Everyone took it calmly for Daniels' sake. That night both Annie and Daniel slept peacefully for they have finally done what they have wanted to do for years. A few months later Annie went to the doctor to see how the baby was progressing and what the gender of the baby is.

"The baby is progressing well but, it's a little hard to tell what the gender is. Come back in two weeks and we might be able to see what the gender is." The Doctor addressed.

At dinner there was a quiet moment so Annie told the family about what the doctor prescribed.

Daniel responded calmly saying

"That's good!"

Then everyone continued eating. That night both Annie and Daniel dreamed about what the gender will be. During breakfast Annie asked her husbands' to make lists' of baby names for both boy and girl. After they all finished eating they started on their lists'.

Boy

Dominic	Jackson	Daniel	Richard	Hayden	Finals
Henry	Edward	Devon	Warner	Peter	Henry
					Edward
					Warner

Girl

Dominic	Jackson	Daniel	Richard	Hayden	Finals
Emma	Bonnie	Marcia	Katie	Alice	Emma
					Bonnie
					Katie

13 days later Annie went back to the doctor to see if they can tell what the gender is. The doctor took a look and announced

"It's a boy!"

At dinner Annie told the family the news. Also Daniel had some news of his own; the doctor said that his heart had completely healed from the heart attack. Everyone was filled with joy with the wonderful news. That night everyone went to bed with a big smile on their faces. Suddenly Annie woke up realizing that she does not have a due date still. When the doctors' office opened she called luckily Dr. Gary Stephens answered the phone; she told him what she realized last night so he told her

"Come in at noon today and we'll see what I can do."

She went and she got what she came for; a due date.

"The baby is doing well; your due date is 2/10/2015!" the doctor announced.

At dinner Annie told the family the due date. Everyone was anxious and happy to know the due date. Once again there was joy and happiness in the air.

Annie had some morning sickness and she rested most of the time and Daniel was doing fine. He was doing what he could to comfort his wife and not to have another heart attack even though his heart healed he can have another one with a lot of stress or he starts smoking again which he kept his promise for he didn't want to put his loved ones through that horrible event again.

The date is 6/16/2014 and Annie is glowing and Daniel is happy the kids are filled with joy and the other husbands' feel like they are in heaven for they have kid(s), a wife, a beautiful home, and a lot of money too. Everyone is happy as can be. The months go by and it's the same everyday Carlie, Bella, and Anakin go to school and Jasper goes to daycare and Jessica stays home for she is 5 months old. It's now October and Halloween/anniversary of Daniels' heart attack is a few weeks away and Annie is worried about what will happen this year on that very day. The day (10/31/2014) has come and Annie is constantly watching Daniel and the other husbands' and Daniel is worried about Annie how her watching him is affecting the baby. Daniel and Annie made a deal that they will lie in his room and watch movies while her head is listing to his heart monitoring the beating of his heart.

The month is now November and it is 3 months till the baby is born everyone is anxious and excited all the time. Carlie, Bella, and Anakin have a school play at the end of the month before their break. All three are nervous about their first play especially since Dominic and Richard are actors and they don't want to disappoint their famous dads'. Both Dominic and Richard try to calm and comfort their kids by saying

"It's ok at first I was bad but, I got better and if you want to pursue the acting career you will get better too. So don't worry at least you are giving my career a try that is all that matters and have fun."

They try to keep that in their minds but, it slips and they go back to the way they were.

Tonight is the play and Dominic and Richard told their kids there last comfort speech before the play.

A half hour later—the play was over and the kids wanted to do it again. Dominic and Richard didn't want to ask if they got scared because it sounds like they had a lot of fun being on that stage and acting before many people too.

It's now December and in two months the baby will be born but, Christmas comes before February so everyone is out getting presents for Annie, Dominic, Daniel, Richard, Hayden, Jackson, Anakin, Carlie, Bella, Jasper, Jessica, and the unborn baby.

Christmas day is here and everyone got 5 presents but for the unborn baby got gifts from the grandparents and more family members.

Chapter 58

the new year

It's now January 3rd 2015 in one month and 8 days there will be a new family member and everyone is anxious and eager especially Daniel for he is the last husband to become a father for the first time; he had waited too long for this moment.

A month later everyone is going crazy for the birth of a new family member is soon in fact 8 days to be exact.

At 11:00 A.M. Annie was beginning to feel contractions. 10 minutes later her water broke. 5 minutes later they arrived at the hospital. 5 minutes later Henry Edward Gresham was born but, not in the hospital; the parking lot of the hospital also the baby was delivered by a registered nurse instead of a Doctor.

Henry Edward Gresham
2/10/2015 at 11:20 A.M.
RN Kayla Radcliffe
London, England
Red Cross Hospital Parking Lot

Both Annie and Henry stayed in the hospital for two to three weeks to make sure that they didn't get any germs from the parking lot in or on parts of their bodies. Both were healthy as can be and they were released two days after the germ results came back. At home Daniel was putting the finishing touches on his son's part of the boys' room he is so excited he's more excited than before. Hayden would not allow Daniel to drive to the hospital and pick up Annie and Henry because he was too happy and might cause a car crash so Hayden drove and Daniel rode in the passenger seat so he would be there for his sons first car ride to home. Hayden and Daniel met Annie with Henry in her arms and took her and Henry carefully to the car and drove carefully home. Daniel Put his son in his personal bedroom and Daniel read a book while Annie slept by his side as he read to himself and Henry's crib was not too far from Daniel's side of the bed. Daniel had a digital camera and he took pictures of this beautiful moment. Dinner time can and Daniel was feeding Henry and Annie was still sleeping. It was now bed time and Annie was still sleeping no one could wake her so Dominic moved her to her room/art room where she had a bed to sleep on when she is sick. Daniel decided to put Henry with Jessica so they would share baby monitor and put Henrys' baby monitor on Annie to hear if she woke up.

The next day Annie was still sleeping so Richard called for an ambulance and they came and examined her

"She's in a comma!" the EMS guy announced.

They rushed her to the hospital. Everyone was on shock they all thought

"She just had a baby how did she go into a comma? the hospital said she and the baby was healthy."

The kids were very upset they didn't want their mom to die Daniel was constantly thinking

"Will Henry really know his mother?" then he busted into tears and collapsed to the ground.

Annie was put onto life support no one lost hope that their loved wife/mother would come back.

The date is now 7/13/2017 today is Annie's' birthday she's turning 24 it has been 2 years and 5 months since Annie went into the comma she is still alive but still on the life support no one has lost hope yet. Carlie is now 6, Jasper is 5, Jessica is 4, Bella is 6, Anakin is 6, and Henry is now 2. Daniel is even more heartbroken by how old their son is and that she has been in a comma as long as he's been home Henry sleeps with him because he does not want to lose his only thing he will have left if Annie dies. The kids see their mom almost every day and think of her 24/7 365 days a year. Every one misses Annie very much including her father he has been calling the house and every one as answered and they have all said the same thing

"She's in a comma or she's still in the comma."

Every time he cries and says a prayer

"My baby girl, please don't die my grandchildren need you and so do your husbands' I still love you even though you hate me please pull through please I'm begging you please."

Many months go by before a decision has been made about Annie's choice to stay on life support or get taken off the the life support and die. The date is now 9/14/2017 and Dominic had made a choice and told the family about it and they all agreed to give her a new drug that could wake a person up from a comma and would never go back into a comma but, there was a 50 % chance to live and a 50 % to die. The next day the hospital gave Annie the drug and after they inserted the drug they took off the mask for the life support and her heart stopped then it started up again! Annie was finally awake and the husbands' were very happy but, the husbands' didn't tell the kids about their decision so it would be a big surprise for them. The hospital monitored Annie and how she is reacting to the drug she was reacting well and the husbands' were very happy to have their wife back. The date is now 7/16/2017 and the husbands' took their kids to the hospital for a surprise of their lives. Annie knew that he kids will be seeing her today but, she was not ready on how much they grew and their ages. They entered the room. They all gasp and Carlie said

"Mommy!"

"Carlie?"

Said Annie.

Her bothers' and sister' were in shock. Carlie headed toward her mother and they gave each other a big hug then Annie asked Carlie how old she was. Carlie answered Annie could not believe how much she lost of her kids lives. Bella and Anakin walked slowly towards Annie and asked her

"Mommy is that really you?"

"Yes it's me!"

Annie replied

They hugged her and then she said their names.

Next it was Jessica Annie barely remembered how Jessica looked but, she remembered her name.

"Jessica?" Annie said.

"Yes mommy" Jessica replied.

They gave each other a big hug.

Then it was Henrys' turn to reunite with his mom but, he was clutched onto Daniels' leg. Daniel picked him off of his leg and carried him to his mother and announced

"Henry this is your mother she woke up from her deep sleep; she is the lady that was sleeping in the pictures on your first moment's at home."

Suddenly he remembered that Annie is his mother because he looked at those pictures thousands times. Henry tried to get out of Daniel's grip so Daniel put him in Annie's lap and she kissed him on the forehead and he said

"I missed you mommy and I really love you."

Annie eyes watered up and gave Henry a big hug bigger than what his older siblings' got because she went into the comma as soon as she rested at home after she gave birth to Henry. Then out of nowhere Henry asked

"I am I the reason why you went into the comma?"

"Sweetie of course no I was weak they released us from the hospital too soon after all you were born in the parking lot of the hospital not in the hospital itself but, I still love you no matter what and that goes the same for your brothers' and sisters'."

Annie has still not asked Henry his age for she thinks it will become a big shock to her. The doctor came in Dr. Salcido came in and updated the family on Annie's condition.

"Annie is progressing well in a week or two she might be able to go home with a nurse in case if anything else happens to her condition."

Jackson agreed with the doctors' orders.

A week later Annie went home but, not by herself she was accompanied with a RN nurse that could stay home with a patient. Annie was put in her sick/art room and the nurse had her inflatable bed and placed it in Annie's' art/sick room she would keep an eye on her. On her first night home Henry asked if he could sleep with his mom and Annie said

"I don't know if you can or not; can he Nurse Mudd?"

"No I'm afraid not but, what I can do is as soon as she wakes up I'll wake you up and you and your mother can talk about how well did and her you sleep is that ok?"

Nurse Mudd asked.

"If you keep your promise then yes it is."

"I will you have my word."

The nurse said. For she felt sorry that Henry didn't meet his mother until he was two years old.

Annie didn't want to sleep that night for she has been sleeping for two years so she thought about what has been going on during the comma that she was in.

The next morning she asked her family one by one about what they have been doing while she was in her comma.

She asked Dominic first

"I've been making decisions about what to do with you and your comma and been taking care of Carlie and helping Daniel take care of Henry and so has Carlie as well."

Then it was Richard's turn.

"I've also have been making decisions with Dominic about your condition and been helping Daniel with Henry and so has Bella and Anakin.

Then it was Hayden's turn.

"I've also been making decisions with Dominic about your condition and been helping Daniel take care of Henry and so has Jasper as best as he could.

Then it was Jackson's turn.

"I've also been making decisions with Dominic about your condition and been helping Daniel take care of Henry and so as Jessica as best as she could.

Then it was Daniel's turn.

"I've been helping the guys making decisions about your condition and the guys have been helping me with Henry and so has the kids well some the best they can do because of their ages.

Then it was the kids turn first it was Carlie's'

"I've been helping Daniel with Henry. I'm in the first grade I'm getting wonderful grades for you I told you my school progress while you were in your comma to try to wake you up.

Then it was Bella and Anakin's' turn

"We've been helping Daniel with Henry. We are now in first grade we are doing wonderful we have also been telling you our progress while you was in your comma trying to wake you up."

Then it was Jasper's turn.

"I've been helping Daniel with Henry. I'm now in Kindergarten and I'm doing well I was trying to wake you up by showing you my artworks while you were in your comma."

Then it was Jessica's turn.

I've been doing what I could to help Daniel with Henry. I'm in preschool I was trying to wake you up by showing you my artworks while you were in your comma."

Then it was Henry's turn.

Everyone has showed me their love and I sometimes could feel your love when the wind blew. I'm in day care and I thought of you every day. I'm very happy that you are now awake when my brothers' and sisters were trying to wake you by showing you their progress the daddy's was crying when we were trying to wake you up but, it didn't work and now here you are you woke up on your own.

Annie was analyzing what her family had told her. An hour later her thought were together. So she called a family meeting with everyone.

"I've been analyzing what you all have told me and I'm sorry if my comma has caused you all stress I'm sorry that all of you had to help Daniel take care of Henry I'm sorry for everything but, I do appreciate what you all tried to do to wake me up I love you all very much."

She starts to tear up so the nurse put her to bed and the family all stepped in and out of her room to watch her sleep. Annie woke up a few hours later and Dominic realized that the stress that comma caused the family was worth the wait for Annie to wake up so Dominic told Annie what he just realized. Her eyes watered up and said

"I love you all very much."

"I know and we love you too." he replied.

That night at dinner Annie looked around the table and she saw everyone was happy to have her back at the dinner table. Annie felt loved. That night she slept well of course the nurse had to wake her up so she would not get a bed sore. The next day after school ended the kids went into their mothers' room and did their homework and showed her their work they did in class. She as proud of her kids for they have accomplished a lot while she was in her comma.

6 months later (1/23/2018) the nurse and the Doctor both felt that Annie does not need the at home medical help so they ended the service and the insurance paid most of the bill and the family had to pay what was left which was not much. Not before long everything was back to normal then things went downhill. On 1/29/2018 Daniel and Dominic were in a car together and got in a hit and run accident both had broken ribs, and leg and a minor cut to the head. They spent two months in the hospital where they had one arm in a cast and one leg in a cast as well and 15 stitches to their heads. They spent two more months in outpatient therapy. They were out on 5/29/2018 of outpatient therapy. Then things went back to normal. Years went by and the kids passed into the next grade year after year.

The date is now 8/13/2022 and Carlie, Bella, and Anakin are beginning middle school, Jasper is in the 4th grade, Jessica is in the 3rd grade and Henry is in the 1st grade. Annie, Daniel, and Dominic are all doing well and everyone's health is well. Annie is now 29 years old, Daniel is 33, Dominic is 44, Richard is 43, Hayden is 36, and Jackson is also 36. Annie is amazed on how much work she as accomplished on the marriage, the kids and the grades that they are in at school, and how happy everyone is. Two weeks later (10/27/2022) Annie got a phone call from the middle school that 3 out of 6 kids of hers attend.

"I'm calling about Carlie Stevens. I'm the principal Mr. Thomas and I have caught her selling illegal drugs with an 8th grader under the bleachers outside. She's suspended for four weeks. You can come and pick her up or she can come home on the bus. As for the 8th grader I have also contacted his parents' and he has been kicked out of my school and will be sent to jail when he arrives home because this is the 3rd time he was caught. If I catch her doing it again she will be kicked out as well."

"Carlie can come home on the bus along with her brother and sister. Thank you for calling me." Replied Annie.

The phone call ended. An hour later Carlie, Bella, and Anakin came home from school. Annie sent Bella and Anakin to their rooms' and Dominic and Annie talked to their daughter. Annie and Dominic gave their daughter pieces of their minds. Carlie stormed out of the house! Annie called around to see if anyone has seen or has Carlie while Dominic told the family that Carlie has stormed out of the house so he split up the family to look for her. Annie was guilty for taking it out on her very hard. 24 hours later no one has found, seen or has Carlie so Dominic called the police while Annie was on Carlie's' bed crying her eyes out. The police came for a picture of her and looked around the local neighborhood and ask the occupants. All asked said no it was too dark to see anything because they have no street lights. Two days later (10/29/2022) they got a trace. Carlie apparently had been hiding in her drug co sellers' room. When the police gave Annie and Dominic the address they rushed to the house and asked about Carlie. When they asked owners' said

"We don't know anyone with that name; my husband and I are the only people living here."

The police added.

"Ms. We has been staking out in this neighborhood and we have seen this girl sneak into the windows here in the front of the house.'

"Well then officer you have my permission to search my home." The owner said.

"Thank you"

Annie and Dominic felt that they have hit a stepping stone on finding their daughter.

The police had men outside and inside of the house every inch was covered with policemen. They reached to the room and Carlie had a gun in her hand. The police told her to put the gun down. She did then the put her hand in her pockets' and pulled out something fast and stabbed herself. She was rushed to the hospital and died as soon as she entered the hospital. Annie went into a depressed mode and was admitted to a psychiatric hospital while she was in the hospital Dominic became a drunk. Three days after she died the family except for Annie and Dominic planned for her funeral she was cremated. Everyone else went to a sad mode but, not as bad as Annie went into. On

11/13/2022 Annie was discharged and Dominic was driving under in influence so he got into a car accident and died on impact he was also cremated. The police called the house and the house called the hospital and told Annie. Annie went into mourning mode and was released the next day in case it was anything serious and it was not. When she got home there was flowers from his fans, his family, everyone else's family, and more people that they didn't know but, loved Dominic. The next day the family went to plan his funeral when the funeral director asked

"Next to Carlie?"

"Yes please." Answered Annie.

The service was packed with all of the actors that Dominic had worked with and many more people the family didn't know. The next day Dominic Andrew Stevens was put to rest next to his only child Carlie Sophie Stevens. Annie was put on close watch by her family. Now Annie has 4 husbands' and 5 kids; her life was different. It is now December 13th 2022 and Annie is finding it hard to buy less presents' than usual. Christmas day is here and there is not a single smile in the house. No one was happy and /or thrilled. Everyone thought about the ones' they have lost, Dominic and Carlie in one year. Annie thought since she has an extra room that one of the girls may want to move in that room. The girls thought maybe when they are older. Annie was comfortable with that answer. The year is now 2023 and Bella and Anakin are being bullied about their sister is dead because of you and so is her dad and more disturbing sayings. Jessica, Jasper, and Henry are having good and bad days with their moods but, they are not being bullied for they are at a different school. The husbands' are depressed and are going to therapy and Annie is too. The months go by and there is a lot of sadness.

It's now 5/15/2023 the school year has ended and the kids have all passed into the next grade. Bella and Anakin will be in the 7th grade, Jasper will be beginning Middle school, Jessica will be in the 4th grade, and Henry will be in the 2nd grade. Annie is proud of her kids and their fathers' are too. The summer was depressing, sunny, and hot. There were one or two smiles. The husbands' drank beers one or two times and the kids mostly slept. Annie was constantly going through the old family albums with pictures of all including Dominic and Annie carrying Carlie and pictures of them when Annie was two years old.

"Those were happy days." She thought to herself then she started to cry.

Chapter 59

another change

While everyone was sleeping that night Anakin caught something he was up all night. Morning came and Annie went to see why Anakin was taking so long. She came into the room and saw vomit all over the floor, Diarrhea covered his bed. He stated that he had a sore throat so Annie got the thermometer and his temperature was 101°! The kids went to school and Annie rushed Anakin to the hospital the doctors' announced that he had Swine Flu! The doctors admitted him to the hospital and they ordered a vaccine that they have not made in over 10 years. The vaccine was close to Anakin but, he went into a uncontrollable faze. He was vomiting and had Diarrhea. They could not insert the vaccine when a patient was in this kind of fazed. The next morning (2/11/2023) he died of having too much diarrhea. His body could not take it anymore. The date is now2/12/2023 and Annie already told the kids about Anakin and they all were now at the funeral home planning his funeral. The next day on 2/13/2023 it was Anakin's visitation. On Valentine's Day Anakin Matt West was put into the ground next to his father/

uncle Dominic and next to him Carlie. Annie was once again depressed but, she also knew that Anakin did not have a good immune system so she knew that he was at rest. Bella was also depressed for she has lost a part of her; she lost her twin brother. Now Annie has been watching Jasper and Henry if they have the symptoms of Swine Flu. Then a day later they both had a temperature of 99.9° and Annie took them to the hospital! They both had strip throat!

"What a relief!" Annie was very relieved for she didn't want to lose another son or another person she loved and cared for. The hospital gave the boys an antibiotic for the throat other than the throat they were well. That night at dinner Bella, Jessica, and Richard all caught something. Richard checked on Bella and Jessica in the middle of the night and took them to the emergency room. They all had Swine Flu luckily the hospital had the vaccine at their fingertips; they all had it injected into them and in 24 hours they would be able to go home. Richard called the house to tell Annie what was going on and he also said

"If we all progress well then you would have to bring someone to drive my car back to the house."

"Ok tell me if anything comes up." Annie ordered.

"I will. I love you." Richard said with an honest heart,

"I love you too and tell the girls I love them too." Replied Annie.

"I will." Replied Richard.

The phone call ended.

That night at the hospital Richard, Bella, and Jessica all got worse even though they all had the vaccine in them. An hour later they were all pronounced dead. It was not long before the hospital called the house and Annie went ballistic. A day later (3/1/2023) Annie told the others' about Richard, Bella, and Jessica then after that Annie went to plan their funeral. The funeral was the next day 3/2/2023 the funeral was beautiful there was flowers from people all over the world who saw Richard on Broadway and the people he worked with on Broadway as well. On 3/3/2023 Bella was put in the ground next to her twin brother Anakin the Richard in the space below Carlie and Jessica in the space Below Dominic. Hayden and Jackson became drunks. On 3/13/2023 Hayden was driving home and Jackson was in the car also drunk from a Pub (bar) and got into an accident. They died on contact. That night Jasper sensed that something was wrong with his dad. The next morning Annie told the family about what happened last night Jasper went into a depression mode while he and his mother was planning his father's funeral. They were both cremated. On 3/15/2023 the funeral was held. An hour later they were put into the ground. Jackson was put next to his daughter Jessica then Jackson next to Hayden. A day later Jasper was admitted to the same psychiatric hospital that Annie was admitted to. Two weeks later Jasper overdosed on the meds he has been hiding. Ever since he was admitted he has been faking taking his pills and he hid them and then one night he took them all which caused the overdose. Annie went ballistic but she calmed down when she took her calming medicine and went to bed. The next day (3/27/2023) Annie went to plan Jasper's funeral. On 3/28/2023 Jasper's funeral had taken place and it was beautiful. The next day (3/29/2023) Jasper was put in the space below Carlie/Richard. All that Annie had left was Daniel and Henry but, Henry didn't have Annie for the first 2 years of his life of Annie was happy to have more time with her last child and her only living husband. Years have passed and no one died Henry got sick but, not serious both parents' were very happy to have a life of their own and Daniel no longer has to share Annie with other men. The years go by and Annie and Daniel are looking back in those old photo albums.

The date is now 10/12/2045 and Henry is 30 years old, Annie is now 52, and Daniel is 56. Henry is now engaged to a girl named Jane Boleyn and they are getting married on 6/6/2046. They have a lot to do in 8 months. They reserved the church, the place where the reception will take place, searched for the dress, find the dress, buy the dress, order the tuxedos, order the cake, the decorations, and more! A few months later they had it all finished with everything all they have to do now is what the day of the wedding to come. The months go by; Henry and Jane receive many wedding presents then something big happened! Henry and Jane went to a fertilization clinic and she became a future mother to 6 babies! All grandparents' were thrilled but, worried about Jane's health but, then Annie thought

"I had 6 kids and I'm fine but, she's having them at once I had my kids a few years apart."

The happy couple received more presents but, not wedding gifts; it was baby gifts! Jane became bigger and bigger and everyone was happy! When Henry knew that he and Jane would become serious he told her about his siblings and his life when he was young so Jane decided that she will name her babies after their dead aunts' and uncles' he loved it and knew that his mother would too. When both expecting parents' knew what they were going to do they told his parents' the next day. Annie was filled with joy and excitement! The day has finally come 6/6/2046 is here! In a few hours the wedding would take place and hopefully a birth the due date is near for it is tomorrow! Everyone was worried if the bride's water will break it didn't at the wedding but, it did at the reception! Everyone was anxious. Carlie Sophie, Edward Henry, Jasper Sky, Bella Rosie, Anakin Matt, and Jessica Sarah Gresham were born on 6/6/2046 Annie was happy that the names of all six of her kids are still in the family! Henry never saw his mother so happy about anything until the birth of his kids' named with the names of their dad's names reversed and their aunts and uncles who are no longer with them. 6 people entered the world and 1 person left the world all on one night. Ronnie Michael died he was 87. His heart just stopped during the birth of his great grand kids. He was buried with his 4 son in laws and 5 if his grand kids; he was in the space below Dominic/Jessica and next to Jasper. The years go by and the grandkids grow and Annie and Daniel are now in the 60s Daniel is now 68 and Annie is 64 and their health is getting worse. Annie has Breast, liver, and pancreatic cancer because her grandmother had it and Daniel has lung cancer because he smoked before Henry was born and then he quit after he had his heart attack then Henry was born and cigarette smoke can stay in your lungs for quite some time which caused the lung cancer. A year later on 2/11/2058 both Annie and Daniel died at the same time and while they were watching T.V. the next day they were found dead by Henry because he called and no one answered the phone so he came over to see what was going on. After the corner announced them dead Henry called Jane and told her the news and their kids were now 12 and they took it well. Henry planned his parents' funeral the next day he put his parents' in a coffin that held two people. They were also buried in the family plot. They were in the spaces below Anakin/ Jackson and Bella/Hayden. The funeral was beautiful Henry read a poem about his parents' lives and it was beautiful.

My Family
By Henry Gresham
My father was an actor and a good one at that.
My mother was a loving mother

She was married to 5 different guys at the same time. She had 6 kids total. One by one they all died first her oldest child my sister Carlie then her dad Dominic Stevens who was also an actor he was good too. Then my brother who had a bad immune system and a few days later His father Richard, twin sister Bella, and Jessica all got the swine flu they were progressing well then something went wrong. Jessica's father Jackson also an actor and another father figure Hayden also an actor both died in a car accident. Then Hayden's son Jasper died of depression. Years later on the night of my wedding to my wife Jane my grandfather Ronnie Michael the man who created my mom's weird marriage died at my reception as soon as my kids entered the world; in memory of my older brothers' and sisters' I named all of my kids after them since I was the 6th child I gave my 3rd son my middle name as his first and my first as his middle. When I was born in the parking lot of the hospital that my older siblings were born in; my mom and I stayed in the hospital for a few weeks to see if we had any germs. We were released two weeks later. As soon as my mom touched my dad's bed she went into a comma. She was in the comma for my first 2 years of my life. My mom thought when it was just us 3 that my older siblings had her for their first years and more so maybe she thought that this was my chance to get those moments'. Her mind was put to rest. She was always looking at the photo albums when she was two that was when my grandfather arranged the wired marriage and then when the big family got started she was filled with joy and now she's really happy she is in the place where all 5 husbands' and my siblings' are I also know she wishes for my family to be there too. Someday soon mom I will be and so will my family I promise but, until then Mommy, daddy, we all love you and will miss you.

Suddenly it started to rain. Henry knew that it was his mother crying.

They were put into the ground 2/14/2058.

The Family Plot

Carlie Sophie Stevens 1/5/2011- 10/28/2022 Daughter of Dominic and Annie Stevens	Dominic "Dommy" Andrew Stevens 6/3/1978- 11/13/2022 Husband to Annie and father to Carlie Stevens	Anakin Matt West 10/5/2011- 2/11/2023 Son of Annie and Richard West and brother to Bella West	Bella Rosie West 10/5/2011- 2/28/2023 Daughter of Annie and Richard West and sister to Anakin West

Richard "Ricky" Mike West 5/6/1978-2/28/2023 Husband to Annie and father to Bella and Anakin West	Jessica Sarah Mason 9/14/2013-2/28/2023 Daughter to Annie and Jackson Mason	Jackson "Jay-Jay" David Mason 5/8/1986-3/13/2023 Husband to Annie and Father to Jessica Mason	Hayden "Haydee" Heath Wright 4/19/1986-3/13/2023 Husband to Annie and father to Jasper Wright

Jasper Sky Wright 10/16/2012-3/26/2023 Son to Annie and Hayden Wright	Ronnie Earl Michael 12/2/1958-6/2/2046 father to Annie Michael, grandfather to 6 kids and great-grandfather to 6 kids	Daniel "Dan-Dan" Devon and Michael Gresham 7/23/1989 -2/11/2058 The Parents of Henry Gresham, Annie-daughter to Ronnie Michael, mother of 6, wife of 5, and grandmother of 6	Annie Amber Michael 7/13/1993 -2/11/2058

Daniel's room	Jackson's room	Hayden's room	Richard's room	Bathroom
				Dominic's room
		Stairs **up stairs**		
Annie's' Room when sick/art room	Girls' room	Boys' room	Kids play room	

Main level

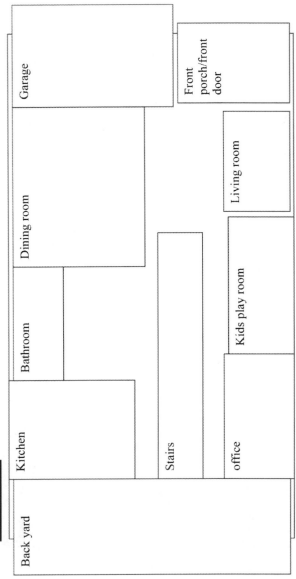

Basement

Bathroom

Stairs